Helicopter Hare

Colin West

Hodder
Children's
Books

a division of Hodder Headline plc

Copyright © 1998 Colin West

First published in Great Britain in 1998
by Hodder Children's Books

The right of Colin West to be identified as the Author and Illustrator
of the Work has been asserted by him in accordance with the
Copyright, Designs and Patents Act 1988.

10   9   8   7   6   5   4   3   2   1

All characters in this publication are fictitious and any resemblance to
real persons, living or dead, is purely coincidental.

A Catalogue record for this book is available from the British Library

ISBN 0340 66095 3

Printed and bound in Great Britain by
The Devonshire Press, Torquay, Devon TQ2 7NX

Hodder Children's Books
A Division of Hodder Headline plc
338 Euston Road
London NW1 3BH

Chapter One

Helicopter Hare is a very rare hare. He has the most amazing pair of ears.

Of course, he uses his ears for listening, like all hares . . .

(Gilbert, Rosemary and Lewis, for instance.) But he also uses his ears for getting about.

When Helicopter Hare (or HH for short) feels in the mood, he spins his ears round, and hey presto, we have lift-off!

This is a useful gift for HH.
He can get over high fences
when others can't.

He can get out of trouble fast.

And he can help anyone else
who might be in trouble too.
This is what he likes doing
most of all.

One day HH was hovering
overhead when he spotted a
hedgehog heading for trouble.

The silly creature was about
to cross a busy motorway,
unaware of the dangerous
traffic speeding by.
"Just the job for Helicopter
Hare," HH said to himself.

He swooped down and plucked
the silly hedgehog from the
dangers of the motorway.
The hedgehog, far from being
grateful, was very angry.

"Gerroff! What's your game?"
he protested as he was
yanked into the air.
"All in a day's work for
Helicopter Hare," replied HH.

"Let me go this minute!"
insisted the hedgehog as he
wriggled about furiously.
"If I did *that*," said HH,
"you'd be smashed to
smithereens on the road below."

The hedgehog huffed.
"OK, then you can take
me to Auntie Maureen's,"
he said grudgingly.

"Auntie Maureen's?" said HH,
taken aback by Hedgehog's
bossy manner. "I'm sorry.
I haven't got time to go out
of my way. I'll just drop you
off on the other side of the
motorway."

"It's Auntie Maureen's place,
or take me back to where
you found me!" insisted the
hedgehog. They hovered a
while in an uneasy silence.

Now, even though HH didn't
much care for Hedgehog, he
could hardly send the creature
back to certain disaster.
It wouldn't be good for his
heroic image.

"This Auntie Maureen, how far away does she live?" HH asked eventually.

"Just the other side of the wood," Hedgehog assured him.

"All right," agreed HH reluctantly. "Just this once, I'll go out of my way."

Chapter Two

Well, although Helicopter Hare's ears are much stronger than most, in truth he can't stay up in the air for terribly long. And after covering half a mile, his ears were beginning to feel very, very weary.

As his ears lost their strength,
so **HH** lost height. The upper
branches of the trees began to
scrape Hedgehog's bottom.
Before long, the bushes and
brambles were doing likewise.

HH had to admit defeat.
"I'll have to land," he gasped
when he could take no more.
"But we're not there yet.
Auntie Maureen lives a good
two miles away. I forget the
precise address, but it's beside
an old oak tree stump . . ."
Hedgehog was cut off in
mid sentence.

SPLAT!

The two of them collapsed in a heap beside a ditch.

"Well!" groaned Hedgehog. "That's one journey I won't forget in a hurry."

"Sorry," muttered HH.
"My ears aren't what they
used to be."
They were *extremely* floppy.
"Give them half an hour to
recover, and they should be
all right."
But his ears showed otherwise.
They were as limp as two
soggy lettuce leaves.

"Look," said Hedgehog, "I'll just make my own way to Auntie Maureen's, thank you very much."

HH was mortified.

In many ways, he would be glad to see the back of Hedgehog. But he mustn't fail in his mission. He couldn't abandon Hedgehog in the middle of nowhere. What would Gilbert, Rosemary and Lewis say?

Call yourself a hero?

Ha ha ha

Ho ho ho

Hee he he

"I'll get you there," HH announced at last.
"But we're lost," wailed Hedgehog. "Totally lost!"
"We'll soon find our way again," declared HH. "Your Auntie Maureen can't be too far away."

Chapter Three

Hedgehog and HH wandered
down a well-worn path.
Suddenly they were
confronted by a whiskery
chap in a chequered suit.
"Good afternoon," said the
stranger slyly.

"Hello!" said Hedgehog,
before HH could stop him.
"You look lost. May I be of
assistance?" the foxy fellow
asked politely.
"We're looking for my
Auntie Maureen," Hedgehog
blurted out, before HH could
stop him.

The fox stroked his whiskers.
"Hmmm . . . Auntie Maureen.
A prickly sort with an apology
of a tail?"
"Yes, that's her!" enthused
Hedgehog, before HH could
stop him.

"I know the way. Just follow
me," said the fox.
"We'd love to," said Hedgehog,
before HH could stop him.

They trudged through the
undergrowth. HH was wary of
the stranger, but Hedgehog
was extremely cheerful. "Thank
goodness *someone* knows the
way," he said excitedly.

When they reached a half
hidden hole in the ground,
Fox turned round. He bared
his teeth in an evil grin. He
was dribbling a bit.

Helicopter Hare spun into action. His ears whirred furiously. They sounded like a circular saw. He grabbed Hedgehog by the scruff of his neck and rose into the air.

They quickly left Fox
far behind.

"Phew! That was a close
shave," said HH. "I was
afraid my ears wouldn't have
enough power for take-off."

Hedgehog was furious.
"But he was about to show us
the way!" he protested.
"*Show us the way?* Come off
it!" said HH. "Foxy was about
to eat us for lunch!"

Hedgehog thought hard.
Those teeth *did* look mighty
ferocious. He had to admit
HH could be right.

They buzzed over the trees until they were a safe distance from Fox's home. HH didn't really care which way. Neither of them had the faintest idea where they were now.

Chapter Four

Suddenly, Hedgehog cried,
"Look down there!"
HH looked. He could see an
accident about to happen.

A day-dreaming mouse was crossing a wooden bridge. The bridge had lots of missing planks, and the absent-minded rodent was looking up at the clouds, humming a happy tune! Another job for HH!

HH swooped down, but
because he was already
hanging on to Hedgehog,
he didn't have a spare hand
for the mouse. He had to rely
on shouting to snap her out of
her dream.
"Cooee!' yelled HH, "Look
out! *Look out!*"

The mouse took no notice.
HH hovered just inches above
her head. In fact, he got so
close that the breeze from his
propeller ears blew off Mouse's
hat. It was only then that she
stopped in her tracks.

And it was just in time.

One more step, and she would have fallen into the river.

The mouse didn't seem at all concerned about her narrow escape. She was much more worried about her hat. It was floating rapidly downstream.

HH had to make a quick
decision. He hovered over the
hat, keeping up with it as it
was swept along. "I'll need
your help," he gasped to
Hedgehog. Hedgehog was
none too pleased.

HH lowered him towards the
water. Hedgehog stretched out
his arm and *just* managed to
grab hold of the ribbon.

HH, Hedgehog and hat
headed back to the bridge,
where Mouse was watching
events eagerly.

They landed on the riverbank
and Hedgehog shook the hat
to dry it off. It was quite wet,
so HH gave it a quick blow
dry with his rotating ears.

Mouse tiptoed over the little bridge, and HH handed her the hat. With a quiet "thank you" she was on her dreamy way again.

"Come on," said HH after a short rest, "we've still got to find your auntie."

Hedgehog clung on as HH spun his ears and took to the skies.

Chapter Five

After a while they came
across a grand house with
a swimming pool. There was
a table with some left-over
sandwiches and green salad.

"This looks tasty," said HH.
"I could do with a bite to eat."
He landed gently on the lawn.

HH licked his lips. There was
nothing he liked more than
green salad. He went over to
the food and started nibbling
on a lettuce leaf.

Hedgehog looked on sadly.
He was sorry to be missing
his tea with Auntie Maureen.
(She always made Beetle
Soup on Thursdays, and
Beetle Soup was Hedgehog's
favourite.)

Helicopter Hare's nibbling was soon interrupted by the sound of heavy footsteps.

"What's goin' on 'ere?" asked a rather frightening voice.

HH almost choked on a piece of cucumber.

"I'm sorry," he spluttered, "we're looking for Hedgehog's Auntie Maureen."

"Well, you won't find 'er 'ere!"
boomed the voice. It belonged
to a huge badger dressed up
as a butler.

"It's been a long day,"
explained HH. "My ears
have gone all floppy. I was
hungry . . ."

"Is that so?" snapped the
badger as he snatched away
the salad.
Hedgehog looked on in
silence. His day wasn't going
at all well.

Suddenly they were joined by
someone else. Someone they
both recognised instantly.

It was none other than Ricky
Afghan, the famous rock star.
They could hardly believe
their eyes.

Ricky spoke in that gruff
voice which has sold so many
records. "Well, howdy. Hey,
I dig your outfit, Mr Hare."

HH was lost for words.

So was Hedgehog. He bit his lip, he cleared his throat, and at last he managed to speak: "We're sorry to have bothered you. We're just on our way to visit my aunt. We didn't mean to intrude. I'm a great fan of yours after all . . ."

HH wasn't to be outdone.
"But I'm a *real* fan," he said,
bowing his head.

Then HH twirled his ears
round - not enough to take
off, but just enough to produce
a refreshing breeze, like a fan.

"Wow, cool!" laughed Ricky.
The butler coughed discreetly
in the background.
"Oh yeah," said Ricky,
nodding at the badger.
"I've gotta be off. I'm doing
a charity gig at Brocklebank."

"Brocklebank?" repeated
Hedgehog. "Hmm . . . that
rings a bell."
Then he snapped his fingers.

"I've got it!" he hooted.
"Brocklebank is where Auntie
Maureen lives! It's all come
back to me now. Oak Tree
Wood, near Brocklebank.
Telephone: *Brocklebank 73838.*"

Chapter Six

Ricky wasted no time.
In seconds he was talking
on his mobile phone.
"Hiya, Maureen. Ricky
Afghan here . . .

 Hey, guess what, your nephew is here with me!

And some guy called Helicopter Hare.

 Is it OK if I bring them over?

GREAT! We'll see you soon, then!"

The badger put on his
chauffeur's uniform, and
they all piled into Ricky's
limousine. They took the
road to Oak Tree Wood.

After several miles, the
landscape became familiar
to Hedgehog.
"This is where Auntie
Maureen lives!" he squealed
in delight.

The limo screeched to a
halt by the stump of an
old oak tree.
"Anyone home?" yelled Ricky.

A lady hedgehog poked her
nose through the foliage.
Her eyes squinted up at the
car. Then Hedgehog appeared
at the window.
"It's all right - I'm here,
Auntie!" he cried.

Auntie Maureen was
unimpressed.
"The soup is ruined," she
moaned. "Where have you
been all this time?"
"It's a long story," replied
Hedgehog.

"Maybe I can explain," piped up HH. He whirled his ears round for effect, but only managed to get them in a terrible tangle.

"Don't worry!" said Ricky. "Just get in, Auntie. You're all coming to my concert!"

Hedgehog was thrilled at the thought of a Ricky Afghan concert, and Auntie Maureen was excited about a ride in a limousine.

HH was exhausted, but he *was* happy. He had completed his mission, and it was nice to give his ears a rest.

And guess who else was at the concert? Gilbert, Rosemary and Lewis. They could hardly believe it was Helicopter Hare up there in the royal box.